Saving the Ice Bear

Written by Susan Price
Illustrated by Cedric Abt

Collins

1 Ice baby

This happened in Scotland's far north, more than a thousand years ago. It is the story of Farbjorn, called 'Fari' for short, and how he found a baby on the ice.

When Fari was eight, there was a hard winter with deep snow. No one left the house for days.
They huddled over the fire, in the smoke, telling stories and playing games. Fari was bored.

Then Father told them that even the sea was frozen and broken ice was piled high in the bay. Fari wanted to see that.

Dressed in his warmest clothes, Fari trudged against the wind to the beach.

There, ice floes filled the bay, crashing and screeching while the wind howled. Fari found the baby, whimpering, on a lump of ice. Taking off his warm cloak, he wrapped her in it and struggled home through the deep snow.

He was shaking with cold when he reached there. The cows in the byre end of the house stamped as he hurried into the warmth.

Everyone watched him unwrap his bundle.
Father and Grandfather stopped playing their game of king's table. Mother came from her loom. They were all astonished by the baby.

Grandfather said, "An ice bear! That wee one must have drifted on ice all the way from Greenland."

"I shall keep her," Fari said, "and call her Snaesyster." That means 'Snow Sister'.

Father said, "A little sister for our Travelling Bear!" Everyone laughed because 'Farbjorn' means 'faring' or 'travelling bear'.

2 Snaesyster grows

Everyone longed for spring. It cheered them to watch Snaesyster and Fari play tug with an old rope. They laughed to see her run after him like a puppy or greedily eat dried fish soaked in broth. Every night, Snaesyster slept with Fari. He loved her, even when she nipped too hard.

Fari taught Snaesyster tricks: to come, stand, sit and lie down. He taught her to count. Holding up a bowl, spoon and comb, he asked, "How many things do I have, Snae?" Snaesyster thumped her paw three times on the floor. Everyone applauded.

Grandfather and Fari smiled at each other. The trick had been Grandfather's idea.

First, Fari taught Snaesyster to thump with her paw when he tapped his foot. Then he taught her to stop when he coughed. When she thumped the right number, he coughed and she stopped.

"Take her to the king!" Father said. "He won't eat on New Year's Day until he's seen some wonder. He'll give you a shipload of gold for Snaesyster!"

"Yes, take her!" Mother said. "She eats too much." Mother was worried about their stored food lasting through the winter. It was running low already.

Slowly, the year changed. The noise of water was everywhere as snow melted. Trees put out bright leaves, fresh grass grew and the animals that had been shut up in dark sheds all winter were set loose outside.

People were glad to get outside too, into fresh air and sunlight. But they were still on short winter rations and everyone was hungry.

Mother said, “We can’t keep that bear through another winter. She’s too big, eats too much – and she’s dangerous!”

“I’ll feed her!” Fari said. He caught fish and rabbits for Snaesyster. It only made her grow faster.

Spring turned to summer and then the leaves changed and fell. Winter was coming again.

Mother said, "We must be rid of that bear. She steals the slaves' food and they're afraid of her. It's not fair, when they work hard. And I have to be so careful with food stores. I can't have a bear breaking into chests and eating half of it."

"I'll teach her not to steal," Fari said.

Father shook his head. "Fari, I'm sorry. I should never have let you keep her."

Fari hugged Snaesyster and she nuzzled him. "You can't kill her! She's my sister!"

His father snapped, "Be sensible, Fari! It's a grown ice bear, not a kitten!"

Fari was sure his father meant to kill his snow sister.

3 Fari runs away

As days grew shorter and darker, the family prepared for the winter by storing food. They dried fish on racks, hung meat above the fire to smoke and cut piles of peat to burn on the fire.

Snaesyster had to sleep in the yard now and Fari saw Father giving Snaesyster hard looks. She had snatched a fish from a slave-girl, ripping her arm with a tooth. Mother had been furious.

Fari made plans. Over days, he sneaked dried fish, bits of hard cheese, flatbread and smoked meat. He rolled the food in spare clothes, hoping that would keep Snaesyster's keen nose from scenting it. He put it all inside a backpack, which he hid in his bed-roll. Every night, he unrolled his own bedding and every morning, he rolled it up again, to make sure that no one found his pack.

On the night he left, he was
scared, but determined.
To save Snaesyster, he had
to take her to the king.
No one would dare hurt
a *royal* bear.

No one noticed that he
went to bed fully dressed.
Fear kept him awake until he
was sure everyone else slept.
Then he rose, took up his pack
and crept through the dark house.

At the door, he stopped
to put on his cloak and
hat and pull on his boots.
It was hard to lift the heavy
bar of wood that kept the door
shut. He dropped one end
with a bang. He held his breath,
thinking he had woken everyone.
But they snored on.
Fari slipped outside.

The yard was moonlit; the shadows deep. Snaesyster came to him, grumbling, and put a cold nose in his ear. The farm dogs watched them but didn't bark.

With Snaesyster following, Fari walked towards the south. He knew that was where the king lived.

No one missed Fari at first. They thought he'd come home when he was hungry.

When he hadn't returned by evening, people noticed Snaesyster wasn't about either. Then they worried.

"Snow is coming in," Grandfather said. "Heavy snow."

All through that cold night, Fari trudged on as snow fell. Snaesyster padded beside him.

Fari walked until he was exhausted. That is easy to say but hard to do.

When they reached the shore of an icy loch, Fari crawled into the shelter of a boulder, out of the wind. He was warmer there, especially when Snaesyster lay beside him. He opened his pack, meaning to share some dried fish with her – but she took the pack and ate everything. When he tried to stop her, she growled.

"Now we have nothing to eat," he said.
Snaesyster didn't care. She slept.

Cold soon came poking through Fari's clothes with sharp, icy points. Grandfather had often told him that falling asleep outside in freezing cold meant you could never wake up.

He knew he should walk on, but he was so tired.
He snuggled close to Snaesyster, closed his eyes and slept.

Grandfather and Father returned to the house with snow melting in their hair and clothing. Mother waited at the door. "We tried," Grandfather said to her.
"The snow is too deep. But the boy is no fool.
He'll take shelter."

4 Jarl Domnall

Harness bells jingled icily as Domnall, the jarl – or lord of the district – rode on his way to spend New Year with the king. Someone ahead shouted, "Bear!"

Domnall rode forward, to see what the trouble was. Beside the track, shining in the dim light, sat a white bear. Domnall's horse shied and backed away.

Some of Domnall's men slid from their horses and circled the bear carefully. Still this strange bear didn't run away. One of the men cried, "It has a boy!"

Domnall dismounted and cautiously moved to the man's side. He saw, between the bear and the boulders, a boy, who stirred, as if waking.

Fari woke in fright to firelight flickering through darkness. Men shouted. Horses stamped. Bells jingled. Snaesyster growled.

A voice said, “Boy, has the bear hurt you?”

Fari knew the voice. Peeking from behind Snaesyster, he saw a crowd of men holding horses and lanterns. Light gleamed on helmets and mail-coats.

In front stood the man who had spoken. It was Jarl Domnall. He often visited Father and Grandfather. Most people liked Jarl Domnall. Father said he was “fair-minded”.

Fari stood up. He stroked Snaesyster, who still growled.

Jarl Domnall said, "You're Bruni Bald-head's son! Why are you here, in this cold?" He pointed suddenly at Snaesyster. "Is this Bruni's bear?"

"She's Snaesyster," Fari said.

"Your sister is a bear?" All the men laughed, their breath steaming in the cold air. The horses, scared of Snaesyster, stamped and whinnied.

"My father was going to kill her," Fari said. "So I ran away."

"Where are you going?" Domnall asked.

"I'm taking Snaesyster to the king for New Year's Day."

"A grand idea," Domnall said. "Your name is Fari, right? Travelling Bear and his Snow Sister. Come on, let's travel to the king before we freeze."

"You're going to the king?" Fari said.

"I'm spending New Year with him." He held out one hand. "Come slowly to me. Don't scare your sister." With his other hand, Domnall unfastened the big brooch holding his heavy cloak.

Fari went to Domnall, who wrapped him in the cloak. It was fur-lined and warm. Behind him, Snaesyster grumbled. She was puzzled.

Domnall lifted Fari on to his own horse and mounted behind him. He couldn't leave the boy to freeze or be eaten by the bear. At his signal, the troop of horsemen moved off along the loch side with an icy jingling of harness bells.

Snaesyster followed them. Where Fari went, she would go.

5 The king's hall

Domnall sent riders galloping ahead with orders, so when they rode up to the tall palisade surrounding the king's hall, the gates were opened. They clattered through the gatehouse into the yard where Domnall dismounted and lifted Fari down. Grooms hurried to take the horses.

Snaesyster trod warily into the yard. Seeing Fari, she followed him as Domnall led him through the streets to a cattle shed. Inside was a strong pen, made to hold a bull. On the straw in the pen lay a calf's carcass, put there on Domnall's orders.

Snaesyster, smelling the calf, gladly hurried into the pen. While she ate, Domnall locked her inside. "She's safe in there," he said. "And we're safe from her."

Domnall then showed Fari the king's residence. The great hall was the biggest Fari had ever seen, with carved and gilded doors and pillars. And there were so many other buildings: small halls where the king's guests slept; a bath house, stables, kennels, henhouses, kitchens, storehouses, workshops ... By himself, Fari would soon have been lost.

In the hall where they were to sleep, a warm fire burnt and food was waiting.

"I dine with the king tonight," Domnall said. "I'll tell him not to fear going hungry tomorrow."

"You can speak to the king?" Fari said.

"He's my uncle. Will Snaesyster be ready to do all those tricks you told me about on the way?"

Fari grinned and nodded.

6 The king's wonder

Fari stood outside the king's hall, shivering with cold and excitement. Snaesyster was at his side. It was New Year's Day.

A maid had washed his hair with lime water until it stood up in stiff white spikes. Domnall had painted his face and hands blue with woad and put a gleaming bronze collar round his neck.

The hall's doors creaked open and Fari marched forward. Snaesyster followed, grumbling.

Inside, people crowded the long tables. Feeling a cold draught, they looked round – and cried out as a strange goblin entered. A halo of spikes shone around its head, gold glistened at its neck and a great white ice bear padded beside it.

Fari led Snaesyster through the smoke, heat and noise towards the king's table. On every side, gold brooches and golden neck-rings flashed in firelight and then were hidden by drifting smoke.

Snaesyster hissed and whined. She wasn't used to so many people climbing on benches, whistling and stamping. But she still followed Fari.

Fari was afraid to look at the king's face and saw only a scarlet tunic and golden rings on a big hand. But Domnall sat nearby, so Fari looked at him. Domnall smiled and nodded.

Fari shouted, "King! I rode my ice bear from the far north so you could eat your dinner early!"

Laughter came from all around, making Fari proud. Snaesyster growled, lowering her head.

Fari called her name and made the sign for her to stand on her hind legs. She didn't do it.

Fari signalled again.

Snaesyster hissed. Fari felt everyone in that great hall, watching and waiting. "Snae, please. Up."

Snaesyster stood. Nearly three metres of ice bear rose through firelight and smoke, towering over everyone. People cried out.

Snaesyster dropped to her paws and raced for the door. People, yelling, ran from her, knocking over benches, scrambling over tables. Snaesyster barged into a table, tipping it over. Screaming people and clattering dishes fell to the floor.

The guards threw the doors wide. Snaesyster ran out into the cold darkness.

The king laughed. "An ice bear hunt! Domnall, you shall have the skin for a bed cover."

Fari ran from the hall, into the dark, calling for Snaesyster.

7 Wave Leaper

Fari found Snaesyster in the pen where she'd slept. She felt safe there.

Domnall soon came. Snaesyster growled at him, so Domnall stayed outside the pen. He took off his cloak and passed it to Fari. "I'm sorry," he said. "That didn't go as well as I hoped."

Fari wrapped himself in the cloak. "I don't care if he is a king. He's not hunting Snaesyster."

Domnall said, "Does Snaesyster have sea legs?" He laughed at Fari's bewilderment. "I keep my ship, *Wave Leaper,* here. Winter voyaging is rough, but ... My Uncle Sven is jarl of Whale Island."

"Can we go now?" Fari asked.

Domnall's men came quietly from the feast hall. He ordered some to ready his ship and others to fetch clothes and food for their journey.

Fari led Snaesyster to the boat. He walked up the plank to board the ship while Snaesyster leapt over its side. The ship bucked when she landed.

Domnall shut Fari and Snaesyster in the tiny cabin under the foredeck. It was a tight squeeze but Snaesyster was happier away from all the busyness on deck. She curled up and slept.

The voyage was short but Fari had never been so sick. *Wave Leaper* leapt, smacked down, rolled ... Snaesyster was sick too and glad to lie quietly in the cabin.

Domnall called them on deck as the sailors rowed *Wave Leaper* towards a green island. It was a windy day of grey skies. Snaesyster stood upright, sniffing the air. Then she jumped over the rowers, over the ship's side and into the sea with a great splash.

Men cheered as she swam strongly to the beach. On land, she shook herself dry.

Jarl Sven had ridden down to meet the ship. He was startled to see an ice bear leap overboard and kept his men well back.

But when *Wave Leaper*'s crew splashed ashore and the bear ignored them, Jarl Sven came down to the beach. He embraced Domnall, saying, "All are welcome, the bear too! Stay until the sea turns to milk!"

8 Whale Island

Jarl Sven had brought spare horses and they rode to his hall. Snaesyster walked beside them. As soon as they arrived, Sven had a cockerel brought and gave it to Snaesyster. She was his friend after that and did her tricks for him. "An ice bear who counts!" he said. "Not the greatest king in the world has that."

Domnall sailed home soon after, promising to tell Fari's family that he was safe. Fari worried that Domnall would be in trouble for stealing Snaesyster away from the king. "I can talk my uncle round," Domnall said. "You'll see."

Snaesyster loved Whale Island. She roamed about and swam in the sea, even catching seals for herself. Occasionally, she ate sheep belonging to farmers, but Jarl Sven always paid for them generously. It was worth it, he said, because no other jarl had an ice bear to bring him luck.

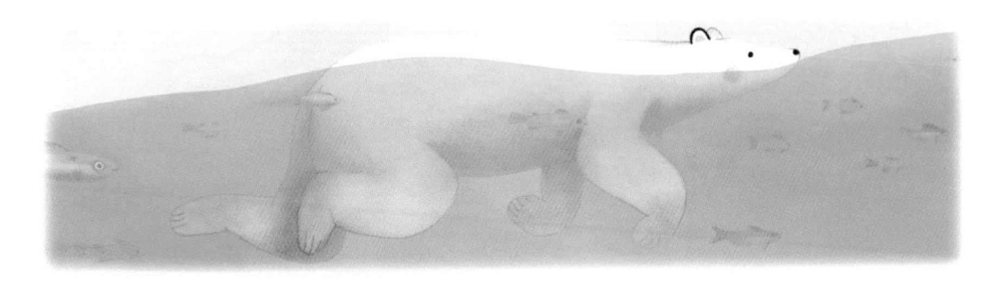

Fari hoped that was true. He and Grandfather thanked Jarl Sven for his hospitality and told him they were returning home on the next ship going their way. Sven wished them a safe voyage and gave Fari a gold armband.

Fari never forgot Snaesyster and often missed her. But she couldn't stay a small, cuddly cub for ever. Bears grow and change, just as people do. You have to let bears and people be themselves, even if it means them leaving you.

So ends the tale of Farbjorn, Travelling Bear, and his Snow Sister.

Fari's journey

 Ideas for reading 

Written by Clare Dowdall, PhD
Lecturer and Primary Literacy Consultant

Reading objectives:

- make inferences on the basis of what is being said and done
- answer and ask questions
- predict what might happen on the basis of what has been read so far
- participate in discussion about books, poems and other works that are read to them and those that they can read for themselves, taking turns and listening to what others say

Spoken language objectives:

- ask relevant questions to extend their understanding and knowledge
- use relevant strategies to build their vocabulary

Curriculum links: Geography – place knowledge

Word count: 2998

Interest words: hard winter, ice floes, byre, loom, loch, palisade, sea legs

Resources: dictionary, ICT for research, pens and paper

Build a context for reading

- Look at the front cover. Ask children to describe what they can see and to explain what they think is happening in the illustration.
- Discuss where this story may be set, what the boy and the bear's relationship might be, and where they could be travelling.
- Read the blurb and challenge the children to predict why Fari is taking his bear to show the king.

Understand and apply reading strategies

- Read the first paragraph with the children, then ask them to raise some questions based on the reading, e.g. *What was it like a thousand years ago in Scotland? Why was there a baby on the ice?*
- Continue to read to page 5. Ask children to recount the events to this point and then to reread this section with a partner to identify any unfamiliar words or phrases, e.g. *hard winter, ice floes, byre end.*